Sir Harry & Lady Frankland of Boston

Books by Ms. Phyllis

Goose River Press
Waldoboro, Maine

Library of Congress Card Number: 2002109291

ISBN: 978-1-930648-41-8

Second Printing, 2019

Published by
Goose River Press
3400 Friendship Road
Waldoboro ME 04572
e-mail: gooseriverpress@roadrunner.com
www.gooseriverpress.com

Sir Charles Henry
Frankland

Lady Agnes Surriage
Frankland

Dedication

In appreciation of the gifted & talented people who have been with me through the years...who have genuinely given their time and support in so many ways...I extend my deepest gratitude... I couldn't have risen to the occasion without that generosity & loyalty...

The sweetest of all being
Mother, Father & Family

Acknowledgement

A special gratitude to the many organizations, individuals, artists and historians, both in the U.S.A & abroad who have contributed their time and talents in assistance during my research years on the Frankland project.

Lisbon, Portugal – Arquivos Nacionais/Torre Do Tombo, Department of Consul & Community Affairs, M. Lewis -Translator, Ministerio da Cultura, Portugal Embassy (D.C.)

Maine – Damariscotta Chamber of Commerce, Lincoln County Courthouse/Registry of Deeds, Nobleboro Historical Society/ chiefly; Dr. George F. Dow, Portland Historical Society, Wiscassett Public Library.

Massachusetts – Abbot Hall, Ashland High School, Ashland Historical Society, Ashland Public Library, The Boston Public Library, Boston State House, The Bostonian Society, The Customs House, Linda's Lovely Dolls, Marblehead High School , Marblehead

Historical Society, The Massachusetts Historical
Society, Senator Clancy & staff, The New England
Historic Genealogical Society/chiefly; Gary Boyd Roberts -
Genealogist, The Paul Revere House, The Post Gazette,
Salem Public Library, The Shirley-Eustis House.

United Kingdom – The British Library, The British Museum,
Chichester City Council, Chichester Museum, Family History
Center, The Frankland Family, The Genealogical Society, The
Maritime Museum, Ministry of Defence/Admiralty Library,
Pallant House/ chiefly; Simon Martin, Ms. Stella Palmer,
Weston Church. NOTE: Ministry of Defence (spelling is correct
according to British records)

The Press – A special thank you to the generous press coverage
in daily, weekly and circular newspapers throughout Maine,
Massachusetts, New Jersey, Washington D.C., and the list
continues to grow. Radio & media coverage has given the
Franklands a voice of notoriety as well.

Memorials

Marion Gosling

Dorothy F. Miles

Dr. George F. Dow

Rose M. Leveille

Stella Palmer/ U.K. Journalist & Author

In recognition for their extraordinary talents,
knowledge & support through the years!
I will always remember all of you fondly.

Special Acknowledgement

To

the Memory of...

Sir Douglas Fairbanks, Jr.

I shall always be grateful for his warm words of encouragement...

a true gentleman and a legend of the Silver Screen...

A SIMPLIFIED FRANKLAND PEDIGREE

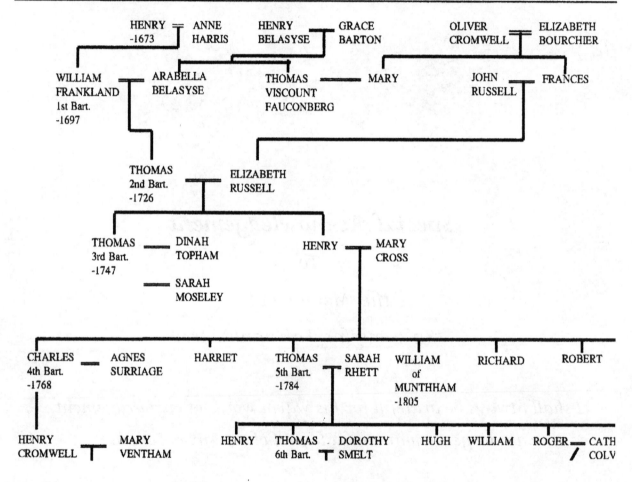

The Frankland Family Insignia
"Free Soil, Free Soul"

Frankland

Preface

It has been said that the thrill of the chase is a propelling force, and truth is stranger than fiction. So true, while forging into the quest of who these Franklands were in Boston's colonial society. Their more than fairytale romance tantalized centuries of authors who have kept the legend alive. I am pleased and privileged to join the distinguished roster.

How often does an authoress, on a getaway weekend in New England, meet her two leading characters, while standing by an old well near a seaside harbor? In fact, the very spot the two encountered each other more than 250 years earlier.

On a brisk autumn day in 1991, this jewel of a romance sparked my curiosity. Ignited perhaps by the same cluster of stars that may have thrusted through the heavens so many midnights ago....the same that brought Harry & Agnes together.
One that has stood the test of time, with a lasting thrill, that never dims...no matter how many times the story is told.

Enjoy! *Ms. Phyllis*

Author's Notes

Author's Notes

After several years of commuting to Boston from my native Jersey, I cashed in the North East corridor tracks to take up residency in Boston's North End. The research would continue spanning over a decade. Probing every archive, library, records office, Universities, or conducting interviews both here and abroad. With the gracious assistance of a list of scholars, professionals, historians, native Bostonians and Marbleheaders. I was met with equally matched talent and hospitality while traveling throughout England & abroad on my journey.

The Franklands were obscure enough, yet well recognized, at least in New England history. Agnes was a native of Marblehead, where her story remained a controversial subject for centuries. Many times raising eyebrows or attracting symposium style lectures...but always turning heads and perking up listeners. Many of the fragmented documents have been preserved in archives throughout New England and abroad.

It was brought to my attention, from sources I am not at liberty to disclose, that there were many well documented official papers concerning Sir Harry and Agnes. Unfortunately, they were destroyed, for one reason or another. With the remaining available sources, retracing their timeline has created a relay effect of written material enabling authors to sort out the facts from fancy of their intriguing story.

My personal method for recanting their story was through a more visual presentation. The best approach, in my opinion, was to create a museum style exhibition. Complete with replicas of the Hopkinton Manor, artifacts and eighteenth century garb. The exhibit traveled extensively for several years. It found a port of call from Washington, DC., on through the eastern coastal libraries and to selected seats of government. Extending as far north as Ottawa, Canada...including the many speaking engagements and symposiums with public audiences.

With the success of the exhibition, it lacked no coverage from the press nor media. It was now evident to me that the tested waters produced a peak of interest, resulting often with the repeated question posed to me, "Is there a book available?"

After 20 years, many thousands of miles logged, and a packed journal full of memories ...without any regrets...I am enthralled to share "Sir Harry & Lady Frankland of Boston" with all of you!

Enjoy! Ms. Phyllis

Illustrations by
Edmund S. Garrett

Table of Contents

Agnes Surriage

The Prelude

*One of the few perfect jewels of romance, needing neither the craft of imagination nor cunning device of word cutting lapidary, is that of Agnes Surriage.

It is so improbable according to everyday standards, yet so calculated to satisfy every exaction of literary art!

*From: "The Three Heroines of New England Romance" / Miss Alice Brown

Charles Henry "Harry" Frankland
Portrait by Annis S. Pratt

* Courtesy of the Frankland Family
United Kingdom

Introduction

In the summer of 1742, Sir Charles Henry Frankland, then Boston's most eligible bachelor, traveled to the enchanted sea-side town of Marblehead, Massachusetts. While conducting stately business on His Majesty's service, the young Custom's Collector alighted to, the Fountain Inn, to seek lodging. There he was greeted at the well, which stood on the property of the Inn, by the loveliest girl answering to the name of Agnes Surriage.

Dressed in the simplicity of her employ as a servant girl, she stood there barefoot, with dark ringlet curls streaming along her cheeks. Her dark deep set olive eyes pierced into his soul from the very first glance.

A moment etched in time that would blossom into a legendary romance, permeating its rose petal fragrance and luster, transcending from the busy tongues of Colonial Boston...
echoing across the pond to Cosmopolitan London.

Charles Henry
Frankland

Charles Henry Frankland

Charles Henry Frankland was born in Bengal, India on May 10th, 1716. His father was Governor of The East India Company at that time. Charles was the great, great grandson of Oliver Cromwell through his maternal lineage.

Upon the death of his father, in 1738, Charles inherited a large fortune. Descending from a pedigree that reached as far back to the *Plantagenet Dynasty, Charles was well connected to the Court. He was offered a choice between Governorship of Massachusetts or the collectorship post in Boston. Harry, as he preferred to be addressed by, chose the collectorship.

He came to the colonies with William Shirley, who then was appointed to the King's Governorship of Massachusetts. Harry's grand welcome to Boston was said to have been celebrated at the Bunch of Grapes Tavern on Kilby Street. Most toasts to British officers were held at the popular tavern.

The Royal Descents of 500 Immigrants

1. Edward III, King of England, d. 1377 = Philippa of Hainault

2. Lionel of Antwerp, Duke of Clarence = Elizabeth de Burgh

3. Philippa Plantagenet = Edmund Mortimer, 3rd Earl of March

4. Roger Mortimer, 4th Earl of March = Eleanor Holand

5. Anne Mortimer = Richard Plantagenet, Earl of Cambridge, son of Edmund of Langley, 1st Duke of York (and Isabel of Castille), son of Edward III, King of England, and Philippa of Hainault, above

6. Richard Plantagenet, 3rd Duke of York = Cecily Neville, daughter of Ralph Neville, 1st Earl of Westmoreland and Joan Beaufort, SETH

7. Anne Plantagenet, sister of Kings Edward IV (d. 1483) and Richard III (d. 1485) = Sir Thomas St. Leger

8. Anne St. Leger = George Manners, Baron Ros

9. Thomas Manners, 1st Earl of Rutland = Eleanor Paston

10. Sir John Manners = Dorothy Vernon

11. Sir George Manners = Grace Pierpont

12. John Manners, 8th Earl of Rutland = Frances Montagu

13. John Manners, 1st Duke of Rutland = Catherine Noel

14. John Manners, 2nd Duke of Rutland = Catherine Russell

15. Elizabeth Manners = John Monckton, 1st Viscount Galway

16. Hon. Robert Monckton (1726-1782), colonial governor of N.Y., British commander in America during the French and Indian wars, d. unm.

15. John Manners, 3rd Duke of Rutland (brother of Viscountess Galway) = Bridget Sutton

16. John Manners, Marquess of Granby = Frances Seymour

16. Lord George Manners-Sutton = Diana Chaplin

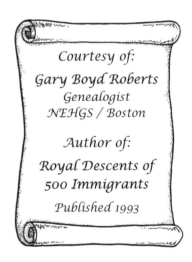

Courtesy of:
Gary Boyd Roberts
Genealogist
NEHGS / Boston

Author of:
Royal Descents of 500 Immigrants
Published 1993

* *The numerical peerage order is exactly as it appears in the Author's Manuscript.*

9

17. (illegitimate by ----) = 17. John Manners-Sutton
    Anne Manners

18. Mary Georgiana Manners-Sutton = Robert Nassau Sutton

19. Mary Isabella Sutton = Sir George Baker, 3rd Bt.

20. Sir George Barrington Baker Wilbraham, 5th Bt. =
    Katherine Frances Wilbraham

21. Sir Philip Wilbraham Baker Wilbraham, 6th Bt. = Joyce
    Christabel Kennaway

22. **Mary Frances Baker Wilbraham** of Mass. = Elliot
    Perkins (1901-1985), educator, master of Lowell House
    at Harvard.

10. Katherine Manners (sister of Sir John) = Sir Henry Capell

11. Sir Arthur Capell = Margaret Grey

12. Sir Henry Capell = Theodosia Montagu

13. **Arthur Capell, 1st Baron Capell = Elizabeth Morrison**

14. Theodosia Capell = Henry Hyde, 2nd Earl of Clarendon,
    brother of Anne Hyde, wife of James II, King of
    England, and uncle of Mary II and Anne, Queens of
    England

15. **Edward Hyde, 3rd Earl of Clarendon** (1661-1723),
    colonial governor of N.Y. and N.J. = Catherine O'Brien,
    Baroness Clifton, see below.

10. Elizabeth Manners (sister of Sir John and Katherine) =
    Sir John Savage

11. Margaret Savage = William Brereton, 1st Baron Brereton

12. Mary Brereton = Henry O'Brien, 4th Earl of Thomond

13. Anne O'Brien = Henry O'Brien, 6th Earl of Thomond, a
    cousin

14. Henry O'Brien, Lord Ibrackan = Catherine Stuart,
    Baroness Clifton

15. **Catherine O'Brien, Baroness Clifton** = Edward Hyde,
3rd Earl of Clarendon (1661-1723), colonial governor of
N.Y. and N.J., see above.

10. Frances Manners (sister of Sir John, Katherine, and
Elizabeth) = Henry Neville, 6th Baron Abergavenny
11. Mary Neville, Baroness le Despencer = Sir Thomas Fane
12. Francis Fane, 1st Earl of Westmoreland = Mary Mildmay
13. Elizabeth Fane = William Cope
14. Elizabeth Cope = Thomas Geers
15. Elizabeth Geers = William Gregory
16. Elizabeth Gregory = John Nourse
17. **James Nourse of Pa.** = Sarah Faunce.

9. Katherine Manners (sister of the 1st Earl of Rutland) =
Sir Robert Constable
10. Sir Marmaduke Constable = Jane Conyers
11. Katherine Constable = Sir Robert Stapleton
12. Jane Stapleton = Christopher Wyvill
13. Sir Marmaduke Wyvill, 2nd Bt. = Isabel Gascoigne
14. Mary Wyvill = Arthur Beckwith
15. Sir Roger Beckwith, 1st Bt. = Elizabeth Jennings,
daughter of Sir Edmund Jennings and Margaret
Barkham, and sister of Act. Gov. Edmund Jennings of
Va., ARD, SETH
16. **Sir Marmaduke Beckwith, 3rd Bt., of Va.** = Mrs.
Elizabeth Brockenbrough Dickenson.

10. Barbara Constable (sister of Sir Marmaduke) = Sir
William Babthorpe
11. Margaret Babthorpe = Sir Henry Cholmley
12. Mary Cholmley = Hon. Henry Fairfax
13. Henry Fairfax, 4th Baron Fairfax = Frances Barwick

14. Thomas Fairfax, 5th Baron Fairfax = Catherine Colepepper (Culpeper), daughter of Thomas Colepepper (Culpeper), 2nd Baron Colepepper (Culpeper), colonial governor of Va., ARD, SETH, and Margaret van Hesse

15. **Thomas Fairfax, 6th Baron Fairfax (1692-1781) of Va.,** proprietor of the Northern Neck of Virginia, d. unm.

14. Hon. Henry Fairfax (brother of the 5th Baron Fairfax) = Anne Harrison

15. **William Fairfax of Va., governor of the Bahamas, president of the Colonial Council of Va.** = (1) Sarah Walker; (2) Mrs. Deborah Clarke Gedney.

12. Barbara Cholmley (sister of Mary) = Thomas Belasyse, 1st Viscount Fauconberg

13. Hon. Henry Belasyse = Grace Barton

14. **Arabella Belasyse = Sir William Frankland, 1st Bt.**

15. Sir Thomas Frankland, 2nd Bt. = Elizabeth Russell, granddaughter of Oliver Cromwell, the Lord Protector

16. Henry Frankland, Governor of Bengal = Mary Cross

17. Sir Charles Henry Frankland, 4th Bt., British consular officer = **Agnes Surriage, known as Lady Agnes Surriage Frankland (1726-1783),** Boston, Mass., social leader.

Bro. 17. Sir Thomas Frankland, 5th Bt., admiral (brother of Sir C.H.) = Sarah Rhett of S.C.

Niece 18. Charlotte Frankland = Robert Nicholas

Gr-Niece 19. Harriet Nicholas = Henry Theodosius Browne Collier, admiral

Gr Gr Niece 20. Gertrude Barbara Rich Collier = Charles Tennant

Gr Gr Gr Niece 21. **Dorothy Tennant** = (1) Sir Henry Morton Stanley (1841-1904), the journalist and African explorer, long an American resident; (2) Henry Curtis.

Agnes Surriage

Agnes Surriage

Agnes Surriage was born to Mary and Edward Surriage in the spring of 1726 in Marblehead, Massachusetts. With only the wages of her father's fisherman's earnings to rely on, Agnes supplemented the growing family's needs by working at the Fountain Inn on the banks of the Marblehead harbor.

Agnes's mother, was formerly Mary Peirce, of
New Harbor, Maine. The granddaughter of John Brown,
who was a successful merchant trader that had settled
into the region of Pemaquid Point, (now in the Lincoln
County) area. Brown had amassed a large tract of land,
which eventually was divided among his grandchildren.
He bequeathed a generous land holding in the name of
Mary Peirce-Surriage. Later referred to as
*"The Brown Claim."

*The Brown Claim/See Symposium Notes

Agnes was only about sixteen years of age, had never attended any formal schooling, but was endowed with natural gifts of charm and beauty. Her lovely singing voice must have kept her company, as she went about her daily chores.

Next to the Inn stood a well... one of the four in the town. Later, it would be immortalized as, The Agnes Surriage Well, on Orne Street.

The Fountain Inn
Marblehead, Massachusetts

In the summertime, the harbor's blue waters
shimmered as those of the Mediterranean, dark
and intense in rich hues. The streaks of warm
Emerald colors flowed over the rigged rocks.

Below the hill, were the
fisherman's huts, their
nets hung to dry in the
sunshine. Old lobster pots,
anchors, and oaken
buckets were tossed about,
with the view of Fort
Sewall not far from site.

The Meeting

The Meeting

Shortly after Frankland took
charge of his duties in Boston,
he set out to erect a fortification
for the defense of Fort Sewall,
in Marblehead.

"again he came riding"

In the summer of 1742, after completing the day's work at the Fort, he was seeking lodging. He came to the Fountain Inn. The many recorded accounts tell that Harry first stopped to the Inn for a cool drink.

The arrows of fate and destiny must have come beaming across the sky, for while he stood at the well, he heard a lovely singing voice. Frankland described it as, "The sound of an angel." As she made her way to the well, the two came face to face.

Both immediately smitten, as though time stood still! The moment would define a new chartered course for the two.

Frankland, now engrossed in the loveliness of her wit and charm, was offered the cool water from the well that he had longed for!

He also noticed that she was barefoot. Taking the liberty of giving her a crown, he instructed her to buy shoes with it.

She graciously accepted.

24

The Second Meeting

The Second Meeting

Thereafter, Harry returned to Marblehead to complete his work on the fortification of Fort Sewall.

Once again, he met Agnes as she busily went among her chores at the Inn.

Again, she was barefoot.

When he asked what became of the crown he had given her, she replied, "I did buy the shoes, sir...I keep them for Sunday meeting."

Charmed by her humble answer as well as her countenance, from that point he began to seek opportunity to meet with her parents and the Reverend Holyoke. Together they devised an acceptable plan to bring Agnes to Boston.

He would provide a formal education including nurturing the discipline of the enhancement of Ladyhood. At Frankland's expense, the carefully executed plan began to culminate into action!

The Arrival
In Boston

Agnes's Arrival in Boston

Upon her arrival in Boston, Harry's arrangement for Agnes's lodging was accepted by a preacher's widow that he had known by suggestion. Agnes would have her own quarters in the house. This residence was recorded as being on *Tileston Street, located in what is known as, The North End.

Frankland provided generously for her lodging as well as the formal studies under the auspices of Master Pelham. In addition, a *harpsichord was purchased so that she could continue her music lessons.

*Tileston Street – Boston's North End
*Harpsichord- Piano equivalency /with richer sound

Agnes at her Piano Studies

*After several years, as Agnes was coming of age... she began accompanying Frankland on his formal engagements in society. Including attending Church services at *King's Chapel, on Tremont Street, where Harry was a Vestre member, owning pew number 20. As expected, Boston society expressed an outrage!*

King's Chapel – on the Freedom Trail/Boston

Kings Chapel / Interior East

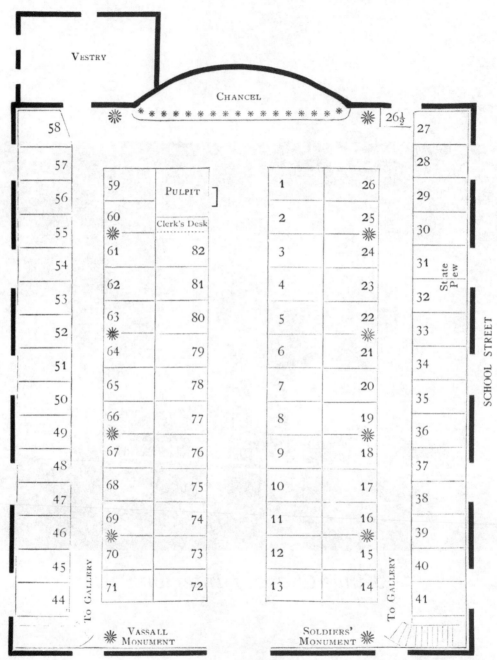

VESTRY

CHANCEL

*   26½

58
57
56
55
54
53
52
51
50
49
48
47
46
45
44

TO GALLERY

59 PULPIT]
60 Clerk's Desk
61 82
62 81
63 80
64 79
65 78
66 77
67 76
68 75
69 74
70 73
71 72

1 26
2 25
3 24
4 23
5 22
6 21
7 20
8 19
9 18
10 17
11 16
12 15
13 14

27
28
29
30
31
32 State Pew
33
34
35
36
37
38
39
40
41

SCHOOL STREET

TO GALLERY

VASSALL MONUMENT

SOLDIERS' MONUMENT

TREMONT STREET.

34

As time went on, more remarkable than her disposition, referred to as : "natural and unspoiled," she always remembered her family and friends of earlier days.

Governor William Shirley's wife, Frances, was chosen at Frankland's request pertaining to the instruction of Ladyhood and refinement. Agnes's studies and progress went exceptionally well.

Social Graces

Of The Eighteenth Century

Upon the death of his uncle, Sir Thomas Frankland, in 1746, Harry succeeded to the Baronectcy. Now, earning the title, Sir Charles Henry Frankland, 4th Baronectcy.

Under the shun from society, Sir Harry thought it best to remove Agnes to a more suitable dwelling location. He purchased 480 acres in Hopkinton, Massachusetts (about 30 miles west of Boston). There he built a twenty-six room mansion where he settled with Agnes, unmarried.

Frankland's family seat was Great Thirkleby Hall in Yorkshire, England. A rich and highly respected family, whose coat of arms bore the motto, "Free Soil, Free Soul."

He was proficiently skilled in several languages, well mannered, eloquent, with interests ranging from botany to literature. Given all of these advantages, he knew that by society's standards, despite his beautiful and accomplished protégé, Agnes, was still deemed unacceptable into the Aristocratic dynasty.

Sir Harry's colleagues from Boston visited them in Hopkinton, but without their wives.

Life at Hopkinton continued. The mansion was furnished in the incomparable high Frankland style. The grounds were embellished with fruit and chestnut trees. Tapestries rich in colors and textures accented the marble trimmed fireplaces, decorated by fluted columns. Gardens and orchards outlined the assortment of floral arrangements delicately.

Special clump boxes with sprays of lavender defined the garden, with a fragrance that Agnes loved best.

Many other luxuries were brought from Europe, as his collectorship post afforded him all the advantages. The two strolled in their colorful gardens daily. Agnes wearing the finest silk attire and brocade, always complimented Sir Harry's wardrobe style.

Their leisure time was spent riding horses, fox hunting, and enjoying each other's company. On quieter evenings they played popular card games, favorably Wist.

Their relationship was in perfect harmony. Complete, with a staff of twelve servants to keep the smooth flow of the magnificent Hopkinton Manor.

Until one day, when a letter arrived from the ancestral home in England.

Duty and Destiny

42

Duty and Destiny

Frankland was summoned home to settle some pressing family business. Agnes became unsettled by this news. She waited patiently for days until Sir Harry finally announced his plan. He soon reassured her that she was to accompany him on the journey across the Atlantic.

Agnes was relieved for a time.

When they arrived to England, knowing fully the task before him, he entered through the pillars of the grand ancestral home. Carefully approaching his Mother, he prepared the family for Agnes's introduction. His efforts were not well received.

As soon as his duties in England were completed, he and Agnes set out on a grand tour of the continent.

Ultimately, arriving to Lisbon, Portugal, where they settled for a time. He chose for them to reside on the eminence of the Seven Hills, among the colony of

other wealthy English.

The Society of Life
in Lisbon

The true motive for his delay in Lisbon was in venture of pursuing a position as Consul General of Britannia based in Lisbon. He wrote two letters in consideration of this request to the King of Portugal and of the Algarves. Soon, the officials in Lisbon were well acquainted with Frankland's Saxon name.

The Letters & Translations to the King of Portugal and of the Algarves

Consul Geral da Naçaõ Britanica
nestes Reinos, Henrique Frankland.

Dom Jozeph, por graça de Deos, Rei de Portugal,
e dos Algarves, &.ª Faço Saber aos que esta minha
Carta de Confirmaçaõ virem, que havendo respeito
a que ElRei Britanico, meu bom Irmaõ, e Primo
nomeou por Consul da Sua Naçaõ na cidade de
Lisboa e Porto deste Reino a Henrique Frankland
pela informaçaõ, que tem da Sua capacidade, ex-
periencia de Negocios, e partes, que nelle concorrem:
Hei por bem, ou que por acto de confirmar, como com effeito
por esta confirmo ao dito Henrique Frankland no
dito Officio de Consul Geral para que o Sirva nesta Ci.de
e Porto deste Reino assim, e da maneira, q.e elle o deve
ser, como, e Servio o Consul Seu Antecessor; assim o
fazem os Consules das outras Naçoẽs Estrang.ras, elle
por Direito o deve ter, e que haja com o d.º Officio os
proes, e precalços que direita.m.te lhe pertencerem, e q.e
goze de todas as honras, privilegios, Liberdades, e fran-
quezas, de que gozaõ naõ os ditos Consules. Notifico-o af-
sim ao Duque Regedor da Casa da Supplicaçaõ, ao
Governador da Relaçaõ, e Casa do Porto, e a todos os
meus Dezembargadores, Corregedores, Ouvidores, Jui-
zes, e mais Justiças, Officiaes, e Pessoas, a quem esta for
apresentada, e o Conhecimento della pertencer, Hei

48

Rey mando e ajam o d.º Henrique Frankland por [...]l da dita Naçaõ nesta Cidade e Portos destes Reinos, o deixem Servir, e exercitar o dito Officio, assim mesmo o fazem os outros Consules das Naçoes Estrangeiras, e elle por Direito pode, e deve fazer, Sem aisso se lhe por duvida, ou embargo algum: E mando que todas as Peroas da Naçaõ Britanica, que residem nesta d.ª Cidade o ajam por Consul della, e lhe deixem uzar do dito Officio, como dito he: e elle jurará em minha Chancellaria de Servir bem, e verdadeiramente, guardando em tudo ao Serviço de Deos, e Meu, e as partes Seu Direito, e do d.º juramento Se fará assente na Carta desta Carta, que por firmeza della lhe Mandei passar, por mim assignada, e passada pela Chancellaria; e pagou de novos Direitos tres mil duzentos quarenta reis, que foram carregados ao Tezour.º delles Antonio Jozeph de Alveira a f.ª 234 do L.º 4.º da Sua Receita, como Constou por hum conhecim.º feito pelo Escrivaõ do Seu Cargo, e por ambos assignado, que foi Registado a f.ª j.º do L.º 12 do Reg.º Geral dos Novos Direitos. Dada em Belem a onze dias do mez de Julho do anno do Nascim.º de N. Senhor Jezus Christo de 1758 = El Rey = Com Guarda = Dom Luiz da Cunha =

Carta porq.ª V. M.ª há por bem Confirmar a Henrique Frankland para q. Sirva de Consul Geral da Naçaõ Britanica nesta Cidade, e [...]

e Portos deste Reino, tudo como acima se
declara = Para V. Mag.e ver =

Por Resoluçaõ de S. Mag.e de 26 de Junho
de 1758 tomada em consulta do Menza do
Dezembargo do Paço = Manoel de Sig.te a foz

General Consul of the British Nation in these Kingdoms, Henrique Frankland

Don Jose, by the Grace of God, King of Portugal and of the Algarves, I make known to those who will read this letter of confirmation that they are to render respect to the British King, my good Brother and Cousin, who has nominated for General Consul of His Nation in the City of Lisboa and Ports of this Kingdom Henrique Frankland, based on the information that He has of His Competence, Business experience, and other qualities. It is my will to confirm Henrique Frankland to the Office of General Consul to Serve this City and Ports of this Kingdom as well and in the same manner that His Antecessor Consul has Served; as do the Consuls of Other Foreign Nations, so, by right, shall he; and that he is entitled to all the powers of his Office, and that he enjoys all honors, privileges, freedoms, and ----- which such consuls enjoy. I will notify the Duke Chief Magistrate of the Casa da Suplicacao, the Governor of the Court of Appeal, and the Casa do Porto, ---- my Chief Judges, Corrugators, Magistrates, Judges, Officials and ----, and whomever the information concerns. I order Henrique Frankland for - - of such Nation in this City and Ports of this Kingdom, and to let Him Serve, and execute such Office, as well as other Consuls of Foreign Nations have done, and He by Right can and should do, without being questioned, or any Embargo: And I order that all the People of the British Nation, that reside in this City, and Kingdoms will have him for Consul, and will allow him use of this office, as stated: he will take an oath in my Chancellery to well Serve, and truly keep everything to the Service of God, and to my service, and the date of the oath will be on the back of this letter, and for the determination of everything I ordered payment, signed by me, and written by the Chancellery; and the payment of new Rights three thousand, (some hundreds), and forty reais (1), that were ---- to ---- Antonio Jose ---- de Moura on ---- 23 the Day of His Revenue, as well as it was verified by the Clerk of the Court of Justice of His (duty) Office, and signed by both, and registered -- 12 of the General Rules of the New Rights Given in Belem to the --- of the Month of July of the armada Birth of Our Lord Jesus Christ in 1758 = The King = With Trust = Don Luiz da Cunha=

Letter by ---- to confirm Henrique Frankland, to Serve as General Consul of the British Nation in this City and Ports of this Kingdom, all that is declared above = To ------
By Resolution declares --- ----- June 26 1758 taken in Counsel by the Honorable Chief Magistrate of Palace (Court) = Manoel de ---

(1) a. Former Portuguese silver coin. b. former unit of the Portuguese and Brazilian monetary system.

TRANSLATION OF ORIGINAL LETTER

51

1759

Monsieur

H. N. 4; Cr 40, H°4 (7)

Les Politesses que j'ai reçues de Votre
Excellence depuis mon Arrivée a Lisbonne, et les
marques de Consideration qu'elle m'a donnees jusqu'a
present, demandoient de ma Reconnoissance que j'eusse
moint tardé a luy en faire mes justes Remerciments, et
je prie Votre Excellence de croire que je n'aurois pas
été jusqu'aujourduy a m'acquiter de ce Devoir si, ma
foible Santé, et mes Incommodités ne m'eussent empeché
de soutenir le mouvement d'une Voiture — mais ce qui
m'a surtout retenu, c'est la Crainte ou j'etois d'interrompre
Votre Excellence dans un tems, ou le bien de l'Etat, et
le Service de Sa Majesté exigeoient tous ses soins. —
Je vous scavois trop occupé, Monsieur, et a des affaires
d'une trop grand Consequence pour vous aller derober
des momens precieux a Votre Souverain et a Votre
Patrie, et que vous avés employes si glorieusement
pour l'un et pour l'autre. —
Actuellement que Votre Excellence vient de Subjuguer

52

le plus horrible Monstre que les Etats ayent a Redouter
et qu'elle a detruit avec tant de Sagesse et d'activité la
plus odieuse Conjuration, je pense que vous avés Monsieur,
quelques Instans de Loisir, dont je suis bien aise de
profiter, pour vous faire mon Compliment et vous
feliciter. C'est bien sincerement que je m'interesse au
Bonheur de Votre Patrie, pour lequel on peut dire que
Votre Excellence travaille sans Relache. —

    Votre Excellence veut elle bien me permettre
aussi de luy rappeller le Souvenir des Requetes que j'ai
eu l'Honneur de luy remettre touchant les Affaires de
Porto, je me flatte que presentement ou Elle est moins
occupée, elle ne desaprouvera point que je la prie d'y avoir
egard: — Et c'est sur les memes Bontés de Votre Excell.
ne j'espere qu'elle obtiendra une Depeche favorable a la
nouvelle Requette que je prens la Liberté de joindre icy
J'ay l'honneur d'être avec la plus parfaite Estime &
Consideration. —

      Monsieur
       De Votre Excellence
        Votre tres humble Serviteur
         A. Frankland

Lisbonne le 25 Fevrier 1759.

1759

Sir,

The kindness that I received from Your Excellency after my arrival in Lisbon, and the marks of Consideration that I have received until today, demand my Gratitude and without delay I would like to express Proper Thanks, and I ask Your Excellency to Believe that I haven't been able to acquit this Duty till today due to my poor health, and to my Discomfort's having Prevented me from enduring of the motion of a carriage - but what has particularly restrained me, is the Fear of interrupting Your Excellency for a moment, where the welfare of the State, and the Service of His Majesty demand all Care.

I know you are extremely busy, Sir, and that your affairs are of such great Consequence that I hesitate to take a few precious moments from Your Sovereign and Your Country, and that You are so gloriously devoted to one and to the others.

At the present time Your Excellency comes from mastering the most horrible Monster that the States have feared and that You have destroyed with so much wisdom and activity the most odious Conspiracy, I hope that you have, Sir, some moments of Leisure, of which I am very delighted to benefit, and to give my Compliments and to congratulate you. It is with real sincerity that I am interested in the Wellbeing of Your Country, for which one can say that Your Excellency works without Respite.

Your Excellency, please allow me to also remind you of the Petition that I had the honor to entrust you concerning the affairs of Porto, I am flattered that since at present you are less occupied, you would never disapprove of the position that I asked you to Consider. - It is the same kindness that I hope for from Your Excellency, and that you will obtain a favorable Dispatch to the new Petition that I take the Freedom of enclosing.

I have the honor of being with my highest Esteem and Consideration.

Sir
Your Excellency
Letters of an humble Servant
H.Frankland
Lisbon, February 21 1759

To Your Excellency
Monsieur Sabastiam Jose de Carvalho e Melo

The Pivotal Destiny

56

The Pivotal Destiny

On the morning of November 1st, 1755...a beautiful sunrise was shining over the city of Lisbon. Frankland, in his court dress, set out in observation of All Saints Day Mass.

Records confirm that he was riding with a companion or acquaintance whom we will refer to as Lady X. She quite possibly may have been well connected politically.

At the hour of 10:o'clock am...before ever arriving at
the service, without warning, the earth surged under
his carriage. A massive earthquake as never before,
struck the city.

One by one, the buildings folded into the raging
sea covering the earth around him.

Frankland lay helplessly trapped. While the companion in
his carriage in terror and agony, bit through the sleeve of
his clothcoat, tearing a piece of flesh from his arm.
She was killed instantly.

Agnes, had stayed behind at their home that morning. In her anxiety, she ran out in search of him in the desolated city. Strange as all of the incidents of her dramatic life, she came upon the very spot of his fearful burial.

She tore at the rubbish covering him with her bare hands. Then offered large rewards to those nearby to help extricate him from the debris. Miraculously, he survived.

It was noted that the fury which enraged the city, might have been a warning to the eccentric, lavish and lustful lifestyle dominating Lisbon. Predominantly, in the quest of their fairy gold and pleasure palaces.

In Frankland's mind, it might have been a sentence for him alone. He waited only until his wounds were healed enough. Then called for a clergy to perform the rite of marriage between he and Agnes

Sir Harry and Lady Agnes returned to England when he was able to travel. While on board His Majesty's vessel, he requested a second marriage ceremony to be officiated by the clergy of the Church of England. Making certain he followed the standard of family protocol.

This time, now introduced as The Lady Frankland, she was received as a beloved daughter by the family.

Soon the two set sail for the colonies. When they arrived to Boston, Agnes was no longer deemed a social outcast. She now walked among Boston society as a princess entering her rightful domain. She gracefully embraced the social scepter of Boston's aristocratic North End.

Sir Harry purchased the twenty six room lordly mansion on Garden Court Street. It had an ascending stairway wide enough to ride his pony up and down safely.

The inlaid floors were designed in Italian marble, trimmed with carven pillars. No less opulent than Hopkinton Manor.

Former Frankland Mansion

Garden Court Street
Boston, Massachusetts

Stairway Hopkinton Manor

Still serving his appointment as the Collector of the Port in Boston...they now spent most of their time on Garden Court. Lady Frankland became a gracious hostess fostering some of the finest social tea gatherings in town. Hopkinton Manor was kept as a summer retreat.

At times, he suffered from the wounds he had endured from the earthquake, but never neglecting his duties. He eventually was granted the Consul General post in Lisbon. Affording them the time to travel between the Colonies and Europe.

In England, he partook of water healing techniques that Bath offered. Hoping to be exonerated of his discomfort and illness. Much of the time with only moderate results. By January of 1768, Sir Harry passed away during his final visit to England. Lady Agnes arranged for his burial ceremony at Weston Church, not far from Bath. He was interred in the Church burial grounds.
*A wooden engraved marker from Lady Agnes was dedicated to his memory.

---

* Engraved marker — see symposium notes

Lady Frankland returned to Hopkinton Manor to live out her days quietly. But, the American Revolution was on the rise. Her association of being a British Officer's widow posed a safety concern. Heeding to warning, she closed Hopkinton Manor leaving at once to make her way to Boston. Although she had a permit of entry into Boston she was detained at the American lines. She appealed to the Committee whereby the Provincial Congress heard her case and appointed six guards to escort her into Boston safely.

The American Revolution now in full peak clearly posed further threat to her safety. In her best interest, she relinquished most of her belongings to set sail for the final voyage to England. She settled in Chichester, living the remainder of her life at Pallant House until her death in 1783.

The Brown Claim Deeds

Original Land Deed From
Captain Somerset to John Brown
July 24, 1626

Somerset
to —
Brown.
Fool. 74
Page 6

To all People whom it may concern, Know ye that I Capt John Somerset and Unnogoit Indian Sagamores they being the proper Heirs to all the lands on both sides of Muscongus River have bargained and sold to John Brown of New harbor this certain tract or parcel of land as followeth, that is to say, beginning at Pemaquid falls, and so running a direct course to the head of New harbor, from thence to the south end of Muscongus Island taking in the Island, and so running five and twenty miles into the country North and by East, and thence eight miles North West and by West, and then turning and running South & by West to Pemaq where first begun. To all which lands above bounded the said Capt John Somerset & Unnongoi Indian Sagamores have granted and made over to the above said John Brown of New harbor in and for consideration of fifty skins to us in hand paid to our full satisfaction for the above mentioned lands: And we the above said Indian Saga mores do bind ourselves and our Heirs forever to defend the above said John Brown and his Heirs in the quiet and peaceable possession of the above said lands. —

Original Land Deed From
Captain Somerset to John Brown
July 24, 1626

In witness whereunto I the said Captain John Somerset and Unnongoit have set o[ur] hands and seals this fifteenth day of July in the year of ou[r] Lord God one thousand six hundred and twenty five. Captain John Somerset his mark and a seal. Unnongoit his mark and a seal. Signed and sealed in presence of us Ma[t]thew Newman, William Cox. July 24th 1626. Cap[t] Joh[n] Somerset and Unnongoit Indian Seigamores personally peared and acknowledged this instrument to be their act a[nd] Deed at Pemaquid before me Abraham Shart. Charlestown December 26. 1720. rec[d] and at the request of Jame[s] Stilson and his Sister Margaret Hilton formerly Stilson they

claimers and Heirs of said lands accordingly entered p[er] hand[s] [Phili]ps one of the Clerks of the Committee for the eastern claims. A true copy examined pr Simon Frost Depy Secy. [Rec]eived June 12. 1810 and entered and examined by Warren Rice, Esq[r]

Land Deed
Captain Somerset to John Brown
July 24, 1626

To all people whom it may concern, know ye that I Captain John Somerset and Urinogoit Indians Sagamores...They being the proper Heirs to all the lands on both sides of Muscongus River, have bargained and sold to John Brown of New Harbor, this certain tract or parcel of land as followeth, that is to say, beginning at Pemaquid Falls and so running direct course to the head of New Harbor, from thence to the south end of Muscongus Island taking in the Island, and so running five and twenty five miles into the country North by East, and thence eight miles Northwest and by West, and then turning and running South by West to Pemaquid, where first begun. To all which lands above bounded, the said Captain John Somerset & Urinoqoit Indian Sagamores have granted and made over to the above said John Brown of New Harbor in and for consideration of fifty skins to us in hand paid to our full satisfaction for the above mentioned lands: and we the above said Sagamores do bind ourselves and our Heirs forever to defend the above said John Brown and his Heirs in the quiet and peaceable possession of the above said lands.

Land Deed
Captain Somerset to John Brown
July 24, 1626

In witness whereunto I the said Captain John Somerset and Urinoqoit have set our hands and seals this fifteenth day of July in the year of our Lord God one thousand six hundred and twenty five & Captain John Somerset his mark and a seal. Signed and sealed in the presence of us, Mathew Newman, William Cox. July 24th, 1626 Captain John Somerset and Urinoqoit Indian Sagamores personally received and acknowledged this instrument to be their act and Deed at Pemaquid before me Abraham Shart. Charlestown December 26, 1720 rec. at the request of James Stilson and his sister Margaret Hilton formerly Stilson. The claimers and Heirs of the said lands accordingly entered in the same one of the clerks of the committee for the Eastern claims. A true copy examined in Simon Frost Department Secretary received June 12, 1810 and entered and examined by Warren Rice, Reg.

Land Deed
From Mary Peirce Surriage To
Sir Harry Frankland
December 19, 1745

Mary Surriage
To
Hon. Franklin Esq.

Know all MEN by these Presents that I Mary Surriage of Marblehead in the County of Essex in New England Widdow for and In Consideration of the Sum of Fifty Pounds Lawfull Money to me in hand paid by *Henry Frankland* of Boston in the County of Suffolk Esquire the Receipt whereof I Do hereby acknowledge and My Self therewith fully Satisfied *HAVE Given* Granted Bargained Sold and Conveyed and DO by these presents give grant Bargain Sell Convey & Confirm unto him the said

Book 27,
Pages 165, 166
at
Registry
of Deeds,
York County,
Alfred, Maine

(Signed
Dec. 19, 1745)

Henry Frankland his heirs and assigns forever All that My
Right Title and Interest of and unto a Tract of main Land and
Islands lying and being at a Place called Misconqus in that
part of New England that Lies between Kenebeck River and River St.
Croix Said Tract Extending from Pemequid falls Eastward and
Northward as far as the utmost Limits Contained in the Original
Sachems Deeds of Said Lands Made to my Grand Father John
Brown and Father Richard Peirce both Deceased which Lye att
Summer Set Cove Broad Bay Round Pond New Harbor or
any other Place or Places Whatever Comprehended within the
Limits of the aforesaid Deeds being one Seventh Part of all the
Said Tract as Described and bounded therein as of right Decend
to Me as One of the heirs at Law to the Said John Brown and
Richard Peirce Together With all Priviledges & appurtenances
there unto belonging or in any Wise appertaining To Have
and To Hold the Said granted & bargained Premisses with
the appurtenances to Him the Said Henry Frankland
his heirs and assigns forever freely and Clearly acquited of and from all
and Other Gifts grants or Incumbrances whatsoever and to warant my
self To have good right full Power & Lawfull Authority to sell Convey & Dispose
of the Same in Manner as before is herein Sett and bounded. And I Do
for my self my heirs and Executers Covinant and Engage to Secure and defend
the Said Henry Frankland his heirs and assigns in the Quiet Peace
able Posession of the Premises against the Lawfull Claimes and Demands
of all Persons holding by or under me forever In Testimony
whereof I have hereto Sett my hand and Seal this Nienteenth Day of
December in the Nienteenth Year of his Majesties Reign Anneque Domini
one thousand Seven Hundred and Forty five — Mary Secveige (Seal)

Signed Sealed and Diliverd. Boston December the Nienteenth one thousand
In Presence of us Seven Hundred and forty five Received of
Peter Preaker the within Named Henry Frankland Esq. the
Nath. Bethune sum of Fifty pounds Lawfull Money being
the Consideration of the within Mentioned Lands from Mary Surbaige
Suffolk ss. Boston Dec. 19 1745. The within Named Mary Serveige
Appeared before me the Subscriber and acknowledged the Within
Instrument to be her Act and Deed Dan. Strietman Justice. Peace.
Boston april 11th 1748 Received and Entred with the Records of
Deeds for the County of Suffolk Lib. 74 fol. 251 &c.

 Exa. Ezek. Goldthwait Regr.
A true Copy of the Original Rec. Apr. 11, 1749 att Dan. Moulton Regr.

105

Henry "Cromwell" Frankland

Henry "Cromwell" Frankland

The couple had no children of their own, however, Henry Cromwell, Frankland's illegitimate son from England had come to live with them in Hopkinton. Later he became, Admiral Henry Frankland, taking his father's name, and serving in the Royal Navy.

Ranks Held By Henry "Cromwell" Frankland

According to <u>The commissioned sea officers of the Royal Navy 1660-1815</u> ed.David Syrett and R.L.DiNardo (Occasional Publications of the Navy Records Society vol.1, Aldershot: Scolar Press for the Navy Records Society, 1994), Henry Cromwell, later known as Frankland, obtained his commission as Lieutenant 6th July 1761; as Commander 10th May 1779; as Captain 14th November 1781; as Rear Admiral of the Blue 1st January 1801; as Rear Admiral of the White 23rd April 1804; as Rear Admiral of the Red 9th November 1805; as Vice Admiral of the Blue 13th December 1806; as Vice Admiral of the White 25th October 1809; and as Vice Admiral of the Red on 31st July 1810. He died in 1814.

A manuscript listing of "Captains and Ships" held here records only one command held by Cromwell: from 25th May 1779 to 22nd September 1781, of HMS *Cabot*, a 14-gun brig sloop, which had been purchased in 1777 and was sold in 1783. Promotion up to the rank of Captain was by merit, but thereafter purely on seniority. It should be possible to trace further information about him through the surviving personnel records of the Royal Navy, in the Public Record Office, Ruskin Avenue, Kew, Richmond, Surrey TW9 4DU: these are described in some detail in <u>Naval records for genealogists</u> by N.A.M.Rodger (London: H.M.S.O., 1988). The log book for HMS *Cabot* for 1778-1781 is also in the Public Record Office, in class ADM 53/149.

Symposium Notes

Symposium notes

Points of references included in the Symposium Notes are merely highlights of the magnitude of endless conversations and opinions my audiences have exchanged in roundtable discussions. I encourage all readers to participate in the challenge.

1. **The Brown Claim** – The land inheritance that was bequeathed to Mary Peirce-Surriage...The property deed is located in Lincoln County, Maine. Spans through several towns, but was never occupied by Surriage. Records show a land deed of the property was purchased by Sir Harry Frankland from Mary Peirce-Surriage.

2. *The reason for **Boston's high society's outrage** against Sir Harry's association with Agnes? Primarily because of jealousy. Many had young unmarried daughters who were available. The thought of such an eligible, accomplished man who wasn't interested in any of them was an insult to their status.*

3. ***Lady X*** – *The companion riding with Sir Harry in Lisbon the morning of the earthquake...was said to have been possibly well connected politically. Perhaps that is true. Would the story have the same outcome if Agnes hadn't stayed back at their home that morning?*

4. *Voltaire's Candide- Poem On Lisbon Earthquake -*
A most in depth poem referencing the magnitude
of devastation describing the effects of the earthquake.

5. *The Redcloth Coat* – The red coat that Sir Harry was
wearing the morning of the earthquake...is described
both in Harry's personal hand written diary and in
Oliver Wendell Holmes's story poem, "Agnes."
Holmes and artist Edmund S. Garrett, actually walked
in the original Hopkinton Manor with all of its splendor.
The testimony of "Black Dinah" who lived on the property
at the time, verbally told that the torn red coat with lace
that she was holding in her hands, was Sir Harry's coat
he had brought back from Lisbon.

6. **The Wooden Engraved Marker** – It is found at Weston Church, England...located not far from Bath. Lady Agnes had the inscription written on a very sturdy dark wooden marker...which is still today well preserved and on view inside the Church building. The services for Sir Harry were officiated by the Reverend Price, affiliated with the Church at the time.

7. **Hopkinton Manor** – Although the original manor burned, another was built on the exact same foundation. Even today, the foundation has endured yet another structure erected on its premises. **Frankland Road**, expands the entire length of the property. Of course, it was granted him from the time he built the manor, and remains the same today. The property line, however, was moved. It is now considered Ashland.

8. Henry "Cromwell" Frankland – Sir Harry's illegitimate son, who came from England to live with Sir Harry & Agnes in Hopkinton. This was perhaps the "Scarlet Secret" of Frankland's past, for the Mother of that child was <u>never</u> disclosed. To this day, its truth remains an unsolved mystery.

Sweet Memories

Sweet Memories
Highlights of Memorable Moments

*Before moving to Boston, the many days & nights waiting on the platform of the Northeast corridor…rain or shine, cold or heat, late or timely, for that Ben Franklin rail to haul it out of the station, in route to Back Bay and South Station. Check in time was whenever I arrived despite any delays. There was always a seat on the train and great Hotel accomodations.

*The first lecture about the Franklands where I was commissioned to speak, was held at the beautiful Jeremiah Lee Mansion, in Marblehead. Despite the torrential rain storm that flooded the streets that morning, by 10 A.M., the white garden folding chairs were filled one by one in the great hall. The attendance superseded the amount of chairs, redirecting the flow of people onto the steps of the six foot wide ascending stairway.

A lovely reception was extended to the guests afterwards.

*The hospitality of so many New Englanders...closest to my affections was, Ms. Marion, historian, history teacher, & special friend. Thank God, for her cordiality...always allowing me the reins to use her home as a "depot" during the erratic schedule I kept through the years. Many times chasing the Marblehead bus #442 back to Boston...until we finally got in front of it...somehow I always managed to successfully board it before it left the last stop in town.

*Another special friend was Ms. Dorothy - English teacher & author...The many wonderful conversations in the grand parlor of her Hooper mansion - once the home of the notorious sea captain, Hooper.

*My walk up apartment on Garden Court Street, in Boston's North End... site of the former Frankland Mansion... the very site that Sir Harry once rode his pony up and down the enormous staircase. (I don't think this was incidental.)

*Perhaps the essence of my labor was expressed best with the welcome of the Frankland exhibition hosted by the Boston State House. A befitting display in Doric Hall on view in the historic structure, whose property once was owned by John Hancock. I ran a bit short on funds that season, originally planning a wine & cheese reception to conclude the celebration.

I opted to forfeit it...since the funds should have been used more productively. On the last day of the exhibition, the end of March 1995...as a strange twist of circumstance would have it...I arrived at the State House about 11 am to spend the day thanking all who made the program possible.

A Citation from Secretary of the Commonwealth, Willam F. Galvin, was in the process to be given me in recognition of the Frankland exhibition. I made a special stop in the governor's office and the Senate Chambers as well.

Suddenly, there was a beautiful orchestra sound coming from the Rotunda in the Capitol. Many of the employees began to congregate around the marble stairwells to listen…So did I.

They were playing a selection of orchestrated Beatle tunes. I was soon made aware that the orchestra was The Royal Marine Band…accompanying the Royals on State visits. The occasion was for England's Prince Andrew's visit to Boston in aide of the American Museum-in Britain. All in all…not a bad exchange of receptions! Ms. Phyllis

A Colonial American Romance

Sir Harry & Lady Frankland

...of Boston

Frankland sites along Boston's
Freedom Trail

Garden Court Street
(Frankland's Boston Mansion-North Square)

Tileston Street
(Agnes's first Boston home-North End)

King's Chapel
(Tremont Str.)

Bunch of Grapes Tavern
(Plaque at Kilby Str.)

The Old State House
(Frankland's Collector's Office)

frankland@embarqmail.com

Map out the Frankland sites
(Along Boston's Freedom Trail)

- **Tileston Street** – Boston's North End
- **King's Chapel** – Tremont Street
- **The Old Custom's House** –
  Originally on the waterfront at Richmond & Ann Street – Later on King Street, near the Old State House
- **The Boston Estate** – Garden Court Street
- **The Bunch of Grapes Tavern** –
  (Plague on Kilby Street)

Bibliography

Brown, Alice
"Three Heroines of New England Romance"
Illustrations by Garrett – 1894

Bowen, Ashley
"The Journals Of"
Colonial Society of Massachusetts, Vol. 1 – 1973

Bynner, Edwin Lassetter
"Agnes Surriage"
Boston, Ticknor & Company – 1886

Crawford, Mary Caroline
"The Romance of Old New England Rooftrees" L.C.
Page & Company

Cushman – Fraser
"Dictionary of American Biography"
Charles Scribner's Sons, 1930

Drake, Samuel Adams
"Old Landmarks & Historic Parsonages of Boston"
Little Brown & Company – 1906

Foote, Henry Wilder
"Annals of King's Chapel"
Little, Brown & Company – Vol. 2 - 1896

Garrett, H.
Paul Revere & The World He Lived In"
Houghton Mifflin - 1942

Holmes, Oliver Wendell
"Agnes"
The Complete Works of Cambridge Edition – 1908

Nason, Elias
"Sir Charles Henry Frankland" or
"Boston in Colonial Times"
J. Munsell – Albany, NY – 1865

Palmer, Stella – U.K. Correspondent
"Portrait of a Lady"
"Dame Agnes Frankland 1726-1783 &
Some Chichester Contemporaries"
Paper from, The Chichester City Council – 1964

Roberts, Gary Boyd – Genealogist, NEHGS, Boston, MA
"Royal Descents of 500 Immigrants to the
American Colonies or the United States" - 1993
"Royal Descents of 600 Immigrants to the
American Colonies or the United States" – 2010

Sanborn, Nathan P.
"The Fountain Inn"
Published by The Marblehead Historical Society – 1921

Slade, Marilyn Meyers
"Agnes & the Knight" – Yankee Magazine – 1963

Voltaire's, Candide (or The Optimist) 1762
Poem on The Lisbon Earthquake of 1755

Ms. Phyllis began a career in broadcasting at PBS in New York City, 1978...where she was granted an internship and held staff positions ranging from scheduling to production assistant with the Emmy Award winning, "Bill Moyers' Journal" program.

Later in 1990 joined MTM Studio & Enterprises in Program Distribution and National Syndication while pursuing writing interests.

Ms. Phyllis studied theatre and screenwriting at the New University (New School) in NYC and earned a degree in Communication.

She received a citation award for a literary exhibition at the Boston State House in 1996—from Secretary of the Commonwealth of Massachusetts, William Francis Galvin, for the "Franklands of Boston" and "Marblehead Cove."

CPSIA information can be obtained
at www.ICGtesting.com
Printed in the USA
JSHW020103160820
7253JS00003B/12

9 781930 648418